The Tale of Cthulhu

Written by Lorenzo di Tonti

Contents

On nights when the moon is full, a small group of high-school friends gather around a campfire near the *Mohegan Bluffs*. On nights when the moon is full, they unleash ancient tales of terror. On nights when the moon is full, they share frightening fables. On this night, the moon is as full as the stories are terrifying. For on this harrowing night in *New England*, Mike Allen will tell a story as old as mankind itself. This particular story has been passed down from generation to generation, with caution interwoven into every spoken word. On this night, they make a call to the old gods. On this night, they make a call to the cult that never died. On this night, they make a call to… *Cthulhu.*

When I was in second grade, I wrote a short story called "The Blob". The Blob was a simple story about my mother making me a school lunch and a young boy who forgot to take it out of his backpack. In fact, he forgot to take it out for the entire school year. There the lunch sat in the bottom of his backpack. While it sat there somehow the mold of the sandwich mutated the sandwich into an evil blood thirsty amorphous blob. After reading the Blob, my second-grade teacher called my mother and accused her of writing the story on my behalf. Apparently, a second grader at a public school couldn't use the word grotesque or amorphous. I mean, at the time I was rather insulted. But, that day, when my second-grade English teacher called me a liar. That is the day I fell in love with writing. I write for the passion of putting words on paper and bringing people a modicum of happiness in their day.

This is Lovecraft like you've never heard it before, told from a bunch of highschoolers around a campfire. One of my initial inspirations for writing, for being an author, was H. P. Lovecraft. The original story of, "*The Call of Cthulhu*" has been told for over *100* years, and there are hundreds of iterations of the same story. To my knowledge, there isn't yet a tale of tale of the tale of, "*The Call of Cthulhu*." As a child I stumbled into the Horror genre, through shows like "*Are you afraid of the Dark*" or "*Goosebumps*" and then eventually the work of H. P. Lovecraft. In the Summer of 1926, H. P. Lovecraft wrote, "*The Call of Cthulhu*", and then published the story in February 1928 in a publication called Weird Tales, Vol. 11, No. 2, p. 159-78, 287. As a quick note to the reader, in an attempt to modernize the original story, there were some deliberate changes to small parts of the original work, such as; character names, word choice, etc. I hope you enjoy reading my homage to, "*The Call of Cthulhu*" as much as I enjoyed writing it.

Publisher: Published Independently on Amazon Publishing and Audible

Pages: 94

Format: Softcover

Word Count: 17200

Publication Date: 8/21/2022

ISBN: 9798847701969

Font: Times New Roman

Font Size: 11

Language: English (USA), Old English (Early 1900s)

Author: Lorenzo Di Tonti

Approximate Time to Read: 2-3 Hours

"Whose turn is it tonight?", Kevin asked curiously to the group of cabalistic campers.

The cramped logs of the campfire snapped, crackled and popped with a ferocious intensity under the translucent white glow of the full-moon. Kevin carefully curated each and every log, like a *Master Chef* handpicking his own berries out of a field. The crackles of the dried-out pine branches flung sparks from the campfire with almost a sentient intelligence. The *icy-chill* of the *New England* air flowed through the campgrounds, like the howling gust of the dust swirling around a Texas tornado. The effervescent glow from the moonlight dimly lit the outer brinks of the campground, like the felt of a *Billiard* table basking under the crystalline beam of a *Neon Bar* sign. The endless rows of arboreous species acted as a natural barrier careening around the campsite. As the fire brewed, the aromatic stench of the beach was drowned out by the fresh scent of pine. The putrid fragrance of rotting seaweed was offset by the refined scent of crisply pruned pinewood.

"I'm up tonight!", Mike Allen said while patiently poking the campfire with a long angular twig.

"Woo-hoo! Great, another insurance horror story?", Kevin asked while squishing his toes deep into the moist sand of the *Mohegan Bluffs*. The sand was as madescent as a full-stack of flapjacks soaked in blackstrap molasses. Kevin was far more accustomed to walking bare-footed around the campfire, like a bohemian prancing around a mulberry tree.

"Oh, no! My deductible! *Argghhhhh*," Deidra said half-jokingly. She waved her hands around and dangled her fingers like a bunch of wind chimes lazily wafting in a breeze. The hazy adumbration from the campfire produced a contorted shadow that danced on her freckly fair skin.

Jon jumped on the dog-pile of verbal barrages and said, "The tale of the Claims Adjuster from… *HELL! Bum. Bum. Bum!* You've been, *DENIED!*"

As the group of friends fondled the fire, they took a second to bask under the brilliant bloom of the Mohegan moon. The moon radiated with a translucent blue that sensuously soaked the campground. This particular part of the Mohegan Bluffs was as secluded as the stories were secretive. So secretive in fact, that even the native New Englanders relied on the use of maps to traverse the local hiking trails.

Mike smirked while poking the logs of the campfire with a misshapen twig. The tip of twig had been worn down by Mike's unrelenting prodding. The twig was firm, yet slim, almost like a diving rod. Mike smiled and concentrated on the smoldering fire, like the myopic trance of a mental patient under deep-sleep hypnosis. He briefly raised his head up, just enough to make eye contact with his friends. The peaks of his brow arched higher than the *Sydney Opera House*. Mike's olive oil skin glistened against the emanating effulgence from the campfire. Mike slowly started to nod his head and said, "We live on a placid island of ignorance in the midst of black seas of infinity, and it was not meant that we should voyage too far. Philosophers have guessed at the awesome grandeur of the cosmic cycle wherein our world and human race form transient incidents..."

Mike paused as a way to solicit feedback from the group. He always found a stealthy strategic pause to be an invaluable litmus test for evaluating the general level of audience interest. He continued prodding the campfire without speaking a word. Pleased by the lack of response, he took a self-congratulatory mental victory lap and continued his story, "*But* it is not from them that there came the single glimpse of forbidden eons which chills me when I think of it and maddens me when I dream of it. That glimpse, like all dread glimpses of truth, flashed out from an accidental piecing together of separated things - in this case an old newspaper item and the notes of a dead professor... I call this story, "*The Call of Cthulhu.*"

"Now were talking," Kevin sharply said with an errant tone of voice. His spirits were as renewed as a teenager learning about the limited duration of his refractory period for the first-time.

Mike abruptly stopped and looked at his friend with a half-cocked head tilt. Four years in a row, Mike was voted, "Most Likely to remain *Class Clown.*" Kevin on the other hand was voted, "*Most Likely to Rule the World.*" Both men came from similar upbringings, working class families in the suburbs, but never surmounted the end of their *Secondary School* experience until *this very Summer*. Around the campfire Mike and Kevin often butted heads, even the most coterminous friendships had their limits. Two Alpha males at the apex of puberty constantly competing for position, like two Rams butting heads to impress an Ewe in hcat.

"*Shhh!*", Deidra scolded her fellow camper. She slapped Kevin on the knee and nudged him with her callipygous curvature. Deidra and Kevin had been awful cozy during the last couple of campfire escapades, but tonight there was an unusual tension between them. Deidra removed her ballcap and started pulling back her hair with long stroking motions behind her head. She pulled out a scrunchie that was hanging on her shoe and put her hair back into a bun. She grabbed the ballcap and squeezed the brim inwards to form an exaggerated crescent moon shape.

"Like I was saying… This is a story, passed down from generation to generation. My grandfather learned it from his great-uncle, he told it to my father, my father told it to me, and now, I'm going to tell it to you."

Kevin pulled out a thermos and charitably offered it up to the group to indulge. Kevin was a people pleaser by nature and always found it most pleasing to bring Hot Cocoa to 'his' soiree. Deidra eagerly obliged by sticking out her hands, like a *Trick-or-Treater* cusping their hands for candy on Halloween. *This* Hot Cocoa was allegedly made from an old Hodges family recipe. I'd later find out from his mother that the secret ingredients were merely just *Rum* and a dash of *Nutmeg*. Kevin was never quite sure whether Deidra showed up for the stories, or for the Hot Cocoa, but either way he appreciated her persistent attendance. Deidra with a cup of cocoa was as bubbly as beauty queen popping bottles of campaign. In our Senior Yearbook, she was voted, *"Most Likely to become an infamous Super Model."* She practically stitched the award into the inner-lining of her lettermen jacket.

Mike continued, "I hope that no one else will accomplish this piecing out; certainly, *if* I live, I shall never knowingly supply a link in so hideous a chain. I think that the professor, too intended to keep silent regarding the part he knew, and that he would have destroyed his notes had not sudden death seized him."

Kevin popped off the lid of the thermos and started pouring some *Hot Cocoa* for his friends. Mike started looking around the camp site for some additional storytelling aides. Mike always found that storytelling wasn't so much about the actual story itself, but how you *told* the story. He stood up with his Hot Cocoa in hand and said, "My knowledge of the thing began in the winter of *1926* with the death of my great-uncle, Kevin Hodges, Professor Emeritus of Semitic Languages in Brown University, Providence, Rhode Island…"

"Really? You put me in the story? Let me guess, I get killed off in some gruesome comical fashion? Or… maybe… *I am Cthulhu!*", Kevin said while seditiously slurping some of the smoldering Hot Cocoa.

Mike loudly scoffed at the comment and continued, "Like I was saying…
Professor Hodges was widely known as an authority on ancient
inscriptions, and had frequently been resorted to by the heads of
prominent museums; so that his passing at the age of ninety-two may be
recalled by many. Locally, interest was intensified by the obscurity of the
cause of death. The professor had been stricken whilst returning from the
Newport boat; falling suddenly; as witnesses said, after having been
jostled by a nautical-looking man who had come from one of the queer
dark courts on the precipitous hillside which formed a short cut from the
waterfront to the deceased's home in Williams Street. Physicians were
unable to find any visible disorder, but concluded after perplexed debate
that some obscure lesion of the heart, induced by the brisk ascent of so
steep a hill by so elderly a man, was responsible for the end. At the time I
saw no reason to dissent from this dictum, but latterly I am inclined to
wonder - and more than wonder…"

Jon raised up his hand and asked, "Lesion of the heart? How'd they
figure that? Seems rather obtuse to just guess that out of the blue…"

"Yeah, how'd they figure that? I thought his death was a mystery,"
Kevin asked to amplify Jon's question.

Mike flung up his hands and said, "Do I come to your work and tell you
how to flip hamburgers? When it's your turn next week, you can tell the
story however you want. Bunch of back seat storytellers…"

Jon pressed his glasses up against the brim of his nose and started
laughing at Mike's delicate sensibilities. His laugh was as hollow as the
belly of a *Coco-Cabana Conga Drum*. He stood *Six-Feet-Three-Inches*

tall and was as skinny as a rail. He couldn't have weighed more than 170 pounds soaking wet. His skin was as pale as freshly laundered linen sitting outside in a Somerville snowstorm. The only blemishes on his alabaster skin were the spots of adolescent acne scattered across his face, like splatters of blood at a crime scene. In our Senior yearbook Jon was voted, *"Most Likely to Become a Ninja."* Unfortunately for Jon, Ninja's were in short-supply in New England, so Jon did the next best thing, he enlisted in the *Marines*. This was probably his last campfire for a while, he was set to start basic-training in about three weeks or so.

Mike looked around the campfire for his cue to continue. Unmolested by any further heckling he said, "As my great-uncle's heir and executor, for he died a childless widower, I was expected to go over his papers with some thoroughness; and for that purpose moved his entire set of files and boxes to my quarters in Boston. Much of the material which I correlated will be later published by the American Archaeological Society, but there was one box which I found exceedingly puzzling, and which I felt much averse from showing to other eyes. It had been locked and I did not find the key till it occurred to me to examine the personal ring which the professor carried in his pocket. Then, indeed, I succeeded in opening it, but when I did so seemed only to be confronted by a greater and more closely locked barrier. For what could be the meaning of the disjointed jottings, ramblings, and cuttings which I found? Had my uncle, in his later years become credulous of the most superficial impostures? I resolved to search out the eccentric sculptor responsible for this apparent disturbance of an old man's peace of mind."

Mike sighed and clasped onto his hot cocoa with both hands. He embraced the cup of molten sugary goodness, like a newborn baby caressing a warm bottle of formula. The ordinarily fresh *New England* air was weighed down by the bellowing smoke plumes exuding from the campfire. There was a madescent quality to the air, like the steam extruding from a dishwasher. Mike grabbed the stick from the ground and started outlining a figure into the sand. The campers peered over the fire to examine the illusive illustration. The drawing was as obscure as a *Rorschach Test* and as legible as ancient Egyptian *sand script*. Mike started to explain the drawing to his fellow campers, like an abstract artist describing his art to attendees at an upscale Brooklyn art-gallery.

"The bas-relief was a rough rectangle less than an inch thick and about five by six inches in area; obviously of modern origin. Its designs, however, were far from modern in atmosphere and suggestion; for, although the vagaries of cubism and futurism are many and wild, they do not often reproduce that cryptic regularity which lurks in prehistoric writing. And writing of some kind the bulk of these designs seemed certainly to be; though my memory, despite much the papers and collections of my uncle, failed in any way to identify this particular species, or even hint at its remotest affiliations."

Mike finished his drawing and continued, "Above these apparent hieroglyphics was a figure of evident pictorial intent, though its impressionistic execution forbade a very clear idea of its nature. It seemed to be a sort of monster, or symbol representing a monster, of a form which only a diseased fancy could conceive..."

Mike started making various hand gestures, like an Italian guy in any given hypothetical situation. He continued with a deep tone of voice, "If I say that my somewhat extravagant imagination yielded simultaneous pictures of an octopus, a dragon, and a human caricature, I shall not be unfaithful to the spirit of the thing..."

Mike daintily draped his hand over to mimic the head of an octopus and said, "A pulpy, tentacled head surmounted a grotesque and scaly body with rudimentary wings; but it was the general outline of the whole which made it most shockingly frightful. Behind the figure was a vague suggestions of a Cyclopean architectural background."

Deidra snuggled up to Kevin as Mike delved deeper into the story. Her head perfectly plopped onto his shoulder, like the snugness of a 3/8-inch socket wrench tightly securing the head of a 3/8-inch bolt. Kevin was more than familiar with the warm embrace of her head, which as of late, was more physical than emotional. Her curly ginger bangs draped over his shoulder, like the tentacles of a giant octopus dangling over a school of fish.

"The writing accompanying this oddity was, aside from a stack of press cuttings, in Professor Hodges's most recent hand; and made no pretense to literary style. What seemed to be the main document was headed **"CTHULHU CULT"** in characters painstakingly printed to avoid the erroneous reading of a word so unheard-of.", Mike said with an ominous disposition.

Mike plunged back down onto the pine log. The log was as rough as sand and as cold as an icebox. He immediately shivered and put his hands up to the fire. After customarily rubbing his hands together, he again polled the audience with a questionable gaze.

"This manuscript was divided into two sections, the first of which was headed "<u>1925 - Dream and Dream Work of H.A. Wilcox, 7 Thomas St., Providence, R. I.</u>", and the second, "<u>Narrative of Inspector John R. Bonilla, 121 Bienville St., New Orleans, La., at 1908 A. A. S. Mtg. - Notes on Same, & Prof. Webb's Acct.</u>"

Mike started perusing the ground for some kind of instructive aide. He quickly scanned the accoutrement for a useable visual prop. On the ground was a local map of the area. Mike snatched the map from the ground and began to fold it back up. He held up the folded map and said,

"The other manuscript papers were brief notes, some of them accounts of the queer dreams of different persons, some of them citations from philosophical books and magazines (notably W. Scott-Elliot's Atlantis and the Lost Lemuria), and the rest comments on long-surviving secret societies and hidden cults, with references to passages in such mythological and anthropological source-books as Frazer's Golden Bough and Miss Murray's Witch-Cult in Western Europe. The cuttings largely alluded to outré mental illness and outbreaks of group folly or mania in the spring of 1925.

The first half of the principal manuscript told a very particular tale. It appears that on March 1st, 1925, a thin, dark young man of neurotic and excited aspect had called upon Professor Hodges bearing the singular clay bas-relief, which was then exceedingly damp and fresh. His card bore the name of Henry Anthony Wilcox, and my uncle had recognized him as the youngest son of an excellent family slightly known to him, who had latterly been studying sculpture at the Rhode Island School of Design and living alone at the Fleur-de-Lys Building near that institution. Wilcox was a precocious youth of known genius but great eccentricity, and had from childhood excited attention through the strange stories and odd dreams he was in the habit of relating. He called himself "psychically hypersensitive", but the staid folk of the ancient commercial city dismissed him as merely "different." Never mingling much with his kind, he had dropped gradually from social visibility, and was now known only to a small group of esthetes from other towns. Even the Providence Art Club, anxious to preserve its conservatism, had found him quite hopeless."

"Sounds a lot like you, Mike," Kevin said while snuggly wrapping his arm around Deidra's shoulder.

Mike smirked and held up both middle fingers. His fingers were as stiff as rigor mortis. Kevin opened his lips as wide as a whale shark preparing to eat breakfast and shot back a shit-eating grin bigger than a Cheshire Cat after a plate full of lasagna. Mike relaxed his hands for a moment and it was evident to the group he had lost his train of thought. His mind was a wander, like an author who forgot to drink his second cup of coffee.

"Now, where was I? Where was I…?", Mike asked with ease.

Deidra interjected the childish show of bravado and said, "I think you were talking about the manuscript."

Mike replied in a sassy tone, "*Ah, yes…* Before I was so rudely interrupted, I was getting to the manuscript… On the occasion of the visit, ran the professor's manuscript, the sculptor abruptly asked for the benefit of his host's archeological knowledge in identifying the hieroglyphics of the bas-relief. He spoke in a dreamy, stilted manner which suggested pose and alienated sympathy; and my uncle showed some sharpness in replying, for the conspicuous freshness of the tablet implied kinship with anything but archeology. Young Wilcox's rejoinder, which impressed my uncle enough to make him recall and record it verbatim, was of a fantastically poetic cast which must have typified his whole conversation, and which I have since found highly characteristic of him. He said, "It is new, indeed, for I made it last night in a dream of strange cities; and dreams are older than brooding Tyre, or the contemplative Sphinx, or garden-girdled Babylon.

It was then that he began that rambling tale which suddenly played upon a sleeping memory and won the fevered interest of my uncle. There had been a slight earthquake tremor the night before, the most considerable felt in New England for some years; and Wilcox's imagination had been keenly affected. Upon retiring, he had had an unprecedented dream of great Cyclopean cities of Titan blocks and sky-flung monoliths, all dripping with green ooze and sinister with latent horror. Hieroglyphics had covered the walls and pillars, and from some undetermined point below had come a voice that was not a voice; a chaotic sensation which only fancy could transmute into sound, but which he attempted to render by the almost unpronounceable jumble of letters..."

Mike reclaimed the stick from before and scratched a jumble of letters into the sand. The letters looked like a random assortment of tiles you might get while playing Scrabble. The letters read, *"Cthulhu fhtagn."*

The group of campers huddled around the fire to observe the mishmash of letters. Everyone was understandably confused by the meaning, let alone the pronunciation. One by one the group attempted to utter the befuddling phrase.

Kevin was first, "Cat-loo-huh fat-nug?"

Followed by Deidra, "Kthhhh...?"

"keth-loo-loo!", Jon proclaimed.

Mike smiled and softly spoke the words, *"kuh-thoo-loo"*.

The group shouted in a staggered unison, *"kuh-thoo-loo!"*

Mike took a momentary victory lap in his head and belayed the continuation of his story as he pieced together the remaining parts. He was putting the puzzle pieces together as quickly as a professional jigsaw competitor at the *Annual American Association of Jigsaw Enthusiasts.* Mike took a second to adjust his sleeveless denim button down vest. In reality, it wasn't a vest at all, it was merely just a denim jacket with the sleeves lazily torn off. Mike had numerous badges glued on to the vest, like *chest-candy* on a highly decorated military uniform.

Mike sternly repeated the word, *"kuh-thoo-loo"*.

His eyes had glazed over, his retinas blackened by the smoke, his nostrils flaring from the agitation of the embers. Mike took in a deep slow breath of the smoke. He inhaled the fumes of the smoke like a dragon breathing in smoldering ashes.

He continued with an expedited pace, "This verbal jumble was the key to the recollection which excited and disturbed Professor Hodges. He questioned the sculptor with scientific minuteness; and studied with frantic intensity the bas-relief on which the youth had found himself working, chilled and clad only in his night clothes, when waking had stolen bewilderingly over him. My uncle blamed his old age, Wilcox afterwards said, for his slowness in recognizing both hieroglyphics and pictorial design. Many of his questions seemed highly out of place to his visitor, especially those which tried to connect the latter with strange cults or societies; and Wilcox could not understand the repeated promises of silence which he was offered in exchange for an admission of membership in some widespread mystical or paganly religious body. When Professor Hodges became convinced that the sculptor was indeed ignorant of any cult or system of cryptic lore, he besieged his visitor with demands for future reports of dreams. This bore regular fruit, for after the first interview the manuscript records daily calls of the young man, during which he related startling fragments of nocturnal imaginary whose burden was always some terrible Cyclopean vista of dark and dripping stone, with a subterranean voice or intelligence shouting monotonously in enigmatical sense-impacts inscribable save as gibberish. The two sounds frequently repeated are those rendered by the letters "*Cthulhu*" and "*R'lyeh*."

"Then what happened?", Deidra asked completely captivated by the creativity of the curious tale.

"Then? Well, then… On March… March 23, the manuscript continued, Wilcox failed to appear; and inquiries at his quarters revealed that he had been stricken with an obscure sort of fever and taken to the home of his family in Waterman Street. He had cried out in the night, arousing several other artists in the building, and had manifested since then only alternations of unconsciousness and delirium. My uncle at once telephoned the family, and from that time forward kept close watch of the case; calling often at the Thayer Street office of Dr. Tobey, whom he learned to be in charge. The youth's febrile mind, apparently, was dwelling on strange things; and the doctor shuddered now and then as he spoke of them. They included not only a repetition of what he had formerly dreamed, but touched wildly on a gigantic thing "miles high" which walked or lumbered about."

"What was it?", Jon asked.

Mike nodded his head as he continued, "What was it? That's a *good* question. Unfortunately, he at no time fully described this object but occasional frantic words, as repeated by Dr. Tobey, convinced the professor that it must be identical with the nameless monstrosity he had sought to depict in his dream-sculpture. Reference to this object, the doctor added, was invariably a prelude to the young man's subsidence into lethargy. His temperature, oddly enough, was not greatly above normal; but the whole condition was otherwise such as to suggest true fever rather than mental disorder."

Mike paused for a moment and downed what was left of his hot cocoa. The warmth of the hot cocoa varnished his throat, giving off this aromatic steam from his mouth as he spoke, like the vapors steaming from a freshly brewed pot of coffee.

"Here's where it gets really weird…", he said while discarding the cup like a cigarette butt quickly being flung from a car window.

"The thing is… the weird thing is… On April 2nd, at about 3 P.M. or so, every trace of Wilcox's malady suddenly ceased. He sat upright in bed, astonished to find himself at home and completely ignorant of what had happened in dream or reality since the night of March 22. Pronounced well by his physician, he returned to his quarters in three days; but to Professor Hodges he was of no further assistance. All traces of strange dreaming had vanished with his recovery, and my uncle kept no record of his night-thoughts after a week of pointless and irrelevant accounts of thoroughly usual visions."

"And… just like that. He was what, cured? C'mon man!", Kevin asked.

Mike smiled and continued unmolested by the question, "The notes in question were those descriptive of the dreams of various persons covering the same period as that in which young Wilcox had his strange visitations. My uncle, it seems, had quickly instituted a prodigiously far-flung body of inquires amongst nearly all the friends whom he could question without impertinence, asking for nightly reports of their dreams, and the dates of any notable visions for some time past. The reception of his request seems to have varied; but he must, at the very least, have received more responses than any ordinary man could have handled without a secretary. This original correspondence was not preserved, but his notes formed a thorough and really significant digest. Average people in society and business - New England's traditional "salt of the earth" - gave an almost completely negative result, though scattered cases of uneasy but formless nocturnal impressions appear here and there, always between March 23 and April 2 - the period of young Wilcox's delirium. Scientific men were little more affected, though four cases of vague description suggest fugitive glimpses of strange landscapes, and in one case there is mentioned a dread of something abnormal.

It was from the artists and poets that the pertinent answers came, and I know that panic would have broken loose had they been able to compare notes. As it was, lacking their original letters, I half suspected the compiler of having asked leading questions, or of having edited the correspondence in corroboration of what he had latently resolved to see. That is why I continued to feel that Wilcox, somehow cognizant of the old data which my uncle had possessed, had been imposing on the veteran scientist. These responses from esthetes told disturbing tale. From February 28 to April 2 a large proportion of them had dreamed very bizarre things, the intensity of the dreams being immeasurably the stronger during the period of the sculptor's delirium. Over a fourth of those who reported anything, reported scenes and half-sounds not unlike those which Wilcox had described; and some of the dreamers confessed acute fear of the gigantic nameless thing visible toward the last. One case, which the note describes with emphasis, was very sad. The subject, a widely known architect with leanings toward philosophy and occultism, went violently insane on the date of young Wilcox's seizure, and expired several months later after incessant screamings to be saved from some escaped denizen of hell. Had my uncle referred to these cases by name instead of merely by number, I should have attempted some corroboration and personal investigation; but as it was, I succeeded in tracing down only a few. All of these, however, bore out the notes in full. I have often wondered if all the objects of the professor's questioning felt as puzzled as did this fraction. It is well that no explanation shall ever reach them.

The press cuttings, as I have intimated, touched on cases of panic, mania, and eccentricity during the given period. Professor Hodges must have employed a cutting bureau, for the number of extracts was tremendous, and the sources scattered throughout the globe."

Mike paused to make his point and catch his breath. In great haste he continued to enumerate the cases, "Here was a nocturnal suicide in London, where a lone sleeper had leaped from a window after a shocking cry. Here likewise a rambling letter to the editor of a paper in South

America, where a fanatic deduces a dire future from visions he has seen. A dispatch from California describes a philosophaster colony as donning white robes en masse for some "glorious fulfilment" which never arrives, whilst items from India speak guardedly of serious native unrest toward the end of March 22-23.

The west of Ireland, too, is full of wild rumor and legendry, and a fantastic painter named Ardois-Bonnot hangs a blasphemous Dream Landscape in the Paris spring salon of 1926. And so numerous are the recorded troubles in insane asylums that only a miracle can have stopped the medical fraternity from noting strange parallelisms and drawing mystified conclusions. A weird bunch of cuttings, all told; and I can at this date scarcely envisage the callous rationalism with which I set them aside. But I was then convinced that young Wilcox had known of the older matters mentioned by the professor."

Mike stood up and outstretched his hands like his savior on the crucifix. Sitting on a log had the benefits of retaining heat from the campfire, but was about as comfortable as wearing concrete pajamas.

"Well, this seems like a good time for a break. Anyone else hungry?", Mike asked while scrounging around in the icebox for a snack. He pillaged the icebox like a bunch of ungrateful relatives rummaging around in unmarked boxes of a deceased relative's attic.

"What do we have here?"

"I brought Smore stuff," Jon said gleefully.

"Whip those bad boys out," Kevin instinctively replied while drumming on his knees.

Deidra bounced up and started happily hunting down some sticks to make the Smores. Luckily, we kept a fresh supply of bundled twigs near the campfire. She rounded up about a dozen or so and balanced them between her arms and bosom. For years, boys never paid her the time of day, then last summer that all changed. That was the summer she turned 18. That was the summer she filled out her figure. That was the summer she turned into a bit of a different person.

The light around the campfire had begun to dim, like the fading ambient of an ebbing candle. Mike and Kevin were too busy assembling the Smore stuff to give it much notice. Kevin would whittle away the sticks and Mike would put the pieces in order. Jon on the other hand had begun looking around for some dry wood to toss in the campfire. After fledging around for several minutes he abandoned the self-appointed task and went to the Barbecue. Jon always kept a spare container of lighter fluid for this very situation. He took the pale container and started spraying lighter fluid all over the campfire. The fire burst up from the ground like an erupting volcano. Instinctively the group covered their faces with an involuntary spasm of the wrists covering their eyes. Mike gently passed a stick to each of his friends. One by one they hoisted the Smore sticks into the campfire.

"How do you like it?", Jon asked his fellow campers.

"Give it to me how I like my chicken! Extra crispy," Kevin said.

"Burnt for me too," Deidra replied.

"You two are perfect for each other, it's rather disgusting," Jon said in jest.

Mike collected the charred remains of the marshmallows and squished them between the graham crackers. The marshmallows bulged out of the sides, like the pudgy belly of a bulky body builder spilling out of his tank top. Mike indecently licked the tips of his thumbs and handed the finished smores back to his friends.

Mike scarfed down his smore, like a hippo devouring a watermelon. He barely chewed the smore, more of an inhaling kind of motion rather than a proper chew. The emulsified marshmallow had the consistency and temperature of molten hot magma. His face turned as bright as a vine ripen grape tomato. He ducked behind the log searching for some water to put out the fire in his mouth. After a second to collect himself, Mike started up again, "Now, where was I?"

He pondered the outline of the story in his head. His eyes moved laterally as he thought through the various aspects of the story. He cleared his throat and said, "The older matters which had made the sculptor's dream and bas-relief so significant to my uncle formed the subject of the second half of his long manuscript. Once before, it appears, Professor Hodges had seen the hellish outlines of the nameless monstrosity, puzzled over the unknown hieroglyphics, and heard the ominous syllables which can be rendered only as "Cthulhu" ; and all this in so stirring and horrible a connexon that it is small wonder he pursued young Wilcox with queries and demands for data.

This earlier expcrience had come in 1908, seventeen years before, when the American Archaeological Society held its annual meeting in St. Louis. Professor Hodges, as befitted one of his authority and attainments, had had a prominent part in all the deliberations; and was one of the first to be approached by the several outsiders who took advantage of the convocation to offer questions for correct answering and problems for expert solution."

A sudden ravage rustling in the bushes caused Mike to abruptly halt his storytelling. The group shrieked as a large foreboding shadow shot out of the bushes. Luckily for the group, the shadowy figure clumsily plunged face first into the sand. Dust plumed into the air like the after-splash from a fat man belly flopping into a public pool. As the dust subsided, the shadow melted away to reveal a familiar face.

"Matt?", Kevin asked.

"Yeah, my bad. I tried to be sneaky," Matt said while dusting himself off. Mike and Kevin ran over to help pick Matt up off the ground. Matt was just shy of *Six-feet* tall and built as sturdy as a *Studebaker*. He was a star running back on the Varsity Football Team. Well, that is until last season when he suffered the receiving end of a 10-man dogpile. His left leg snapped harder than a rusty mouse trap. The surgeon ended up giving him six steel pins in his leg and the crushing news of his 'early' retirement from *Football*. Luckily for Matt, he had a good head on those massive bowling balls he called shoulders. Matt was just as surprised as the rest of us to hear that he was voted, "*Most Likely to Become a Motivational Speaker.*"

"What'd I miss?", he asked the group of friends.

Mike responded with a smile, "We're just getting to the good part. The *Call of Cthulhu…*"

"Awesome. Whose on deck?", he asked while plucking an overdone marshmallow from the fire. Matt played hot-potato with the sweltering marshmallow from the fire. He popped it onto a graham cracker and started to lick his fingers. He walked over to Jon and gave him a quick side hug. Deidra snapped up from her seat and lunged over to Matt. The two exuberantly embraced for a long-overdue hug. Over the years, Matt helped her family out with odd-jobs at their farm and occasionally kept the overly rowdy wranglers in-line.

Mike raised his hands up like a minister giving a sermon and continued, "The chief of these outsiders, and in a short time the focus of interest for the entire meeting, was a commonplace-looking middle-aged man who had travelled all the way from New Orleans for certain special information unobtainable from any local source. His name, his name was John Raymond Bonilla, and he was by profession an Inspector of Police. With him he bore the subject of his visit, a grotesque, repulsive, and apparently very ancient stone statuette whose origin he was at a loss to determine. It must not be fancied that Inspector Bonilla had the least interest in archaeology. On the contrary, his wish for enlightenment was prompted by purely professional considerations. The statuette, idol, fetish, or whatever it was, had been captured some months before in the wooded swamps south of New Orleans during a raid on a supposed voodoo meeting; and so singular and hideous were the rites connected with it, that the police could not but realize that they had stumbled on a dark cult totally unknown to them, and infinitely more diabolic than even the blackest of the African voodoo circles. Of its origin, apart from the erratic and unbelievable tales extorted from the captured members, absolutely nothing was to be discovered; hence the anxiety of the police for any antiquarian lore which might help them to place the frightful symbol, and through it track down the cult to its fountain-head.

Inspector Bonilla was scarcely prepared for the sensation which his offering created. One sight of the thing had been enough to throw the assembled men of science into a state of tense excitement, and they lost no time in crowding around him to gaze at the diminutive figure whose utter strangeness and air of genuinely abysmal antiquity hinted so potently at unopened and archaic vistas. No recognized school of sculpture had animated this terrible object, yet centuries and even thousands of years seemed recorded in its dim and greenish surface of unplaceable stone.

The figure, which was finally passed slowly from man to man for close and careful study, was between seven and eight inches in height, and of exquisitely artistic workmanship. It represented a monster of vaguely anthropoid outline, but with an octopus-like head whose face was a mass of feelers, a scaly, rubbery-looking body, prodigious claws on hind and fore feet, and long, narrow wings behind. This thing, which seemed instinct with a fearsome and unnatural malignancy, was of a somewhat bloated corpulence, and squatted evilly on a rectangular block or pedestal covered with undecipherable characters. The tips of the wings touched the back edge of the block, the seat occupied the center, whilst the long, curved claws of the doubled-up, crouching hind legs gripped the front edge and extended a quarter of the way down toward the bottom of the pedestal. The cephalopod head was bent forward, so that the ends of the facial feelers brushed the backs of huge fore paws which clasped the croucher's elevated knees. The aspect of the whole was abnormally life-like, and the more subtly fearful because its source was so totally unknown. Its vast, awesome, and incalculable age was unmistakable; yet not one link did it shew with any known type of art belonging to civilization's youth - or indeed to any other time. Totally separate and apart, its very material was a mystery; for the soapy, greenish-black stone with its golden or iridescent flecks and striations resembled nothing familiar to geology or mineralogy. The characters along the base were equally baffling; and no member present, despite a representation of half the world's expert learning in this field, could form the least notion of even their remotest linguistic kinship. They, like the subject and material, belonged to something horribly remote and distinct from mankind as we know it. something frightfully suggestive of old and unhallowed cycles of life in which our world and our conceptions have no part.

And yet, as the members severally shook their heads and confessed defeat at the Inspector's problem, there was one man in that gathering who suspected a touch of bizarre familiarity in the monstrous shape and writing, and who presently told with some diffidence of the odd trifle he knew. This person was the late William Channing Webb, Professor of Anthropology in Princeton University, and an explorer of no slight note. Professor Webb had been engaged, forty-eight years before, in a tour of Greenland and Iceland in search of some Runic inscriptions which he failed to unearth; and whilst high up on the West Greenland coast had encountered a singular tribe or cult of degenerate Esquimaux whose religion, a curious form of devil-worship, chilled him with its deliberate bloodthirstiness and repulsiveness. It was a faith of which other Esquimaux knew little, and which they mentioned only with shudders, saying that it had come down from horribly ancient axons before ever the world was made. Besides nameless rites and human sacrifices there were certain queer hereditary rituals addressed to a supreme elder devil; and of this Professor Webb had taken a careful phonetic copy from an aged angekok or wizard-priest, expressing the sounds in Roman letters as best he knew how. But just now of prime significance was the fetish which this cult had cherished, and around which they danced when the aurora leaped high over the ice cliffs. It was, the professor stated, a very crude bas-relief of stone, comprising a hideous picture and some cryptic writing. And so far as he could tell, it was a rough parallel in all essential features of the bestial thing now lying before the meeting.

This data, received with suspense and astonishment by the assembled members, proved doubly exciting to Inspector Bonilla; and he began at once to ply his informant with questions. Having noted and copied an oral ritual among the swamp cult-worshippers his men had arrested, he besought the professor to remember as best he might the syllables taken down amongst the diabolist Esquimaux. There then followed an exhaustive comparison of details, and a moment of really awed silence when both detective and scientist agreed on the virtual identity of the phrase common to two hellish rituals so many worlds of distance apart. What, in substance, both the Esquimaux wizards and the Louisiana swamp-priests had chanted to their kindred idols was something very like this: the word-divisions being guessed at from traditional breaks in the phrase as chanted aloud:

"Ph'nglui mglw'nafh Cthulhu R'lyeh wgah'nagl fhtagn."

Bonilla had one point in advance of Professor Webb, for several among his mongrel prisoners had repeated to him what older celebrants had told them the words meant. This text, as given, ran something like this:

"In his house at R'lyeh dead Cthulhu waits dreaming."

And now, in response to a general and urgent demand, Inspector Bonilla related as fully as possible his experience with the swamp worshippers; telling a story to which I could see my uncle attached profound significance. It savored of the wildest dreams of myth-maker and philosopher, and disclosed an astonishing degree of cosmic imagination among such half-castes and pariahs as might be least expected to possess it.

On November 1st, 1907, there had come to the New Orleans police a frantic summons from the swamp and lagoon country to the south. The squatters there, mostly primitive but good-natured descendants of Lafitte's men, were in the grip of stark terror from an unknown thing which had stolen upon them in the night. It was voodoo, apparently, but voodoo of a more terrible sort than they had ever known; and some of their women and children had disappeared since the malevolent tom-tom had begun its incessant beating far within the black haunted woods where no dweller ventured. There were insane shouts and harrowing screams, soul-chilling chants and dancing devil-flames; and, the frightened messenger added, the people could stand it no more.

So a body of twenty police, filling two carriages and an automobile, had set out in the late afternoon with the shivering squatter as a guide. At the end of the passable road they alighted, and for miles splashed on in silence through the terrible cypress woods where day never came. Ugly roots and malignant hanging nooses of Spanish moss beset them, and now and then a pile of dank stones or fragment of a rotting wall intensified by its hint of morbid habitation a depression which every malformed tree and every fungous islet combined to create. At length the squatter settlement, a miserable huddle of huts, hove in sight; and hysterical dwellers ran out to cluster around the group of bobbing lanterns. The muffled beat of tom-toms was now faintly audible far, far ahead; and a curdling shriek came at infrequent intervals when the wind shifted. A reddish glare, too, seemed to filter through pale undergrowth beyond the endless avenues of forest night. Reluctant even to be left alone again, each one of the cowed squatters refused point-blank to advance another inch toward the scene of unholy worship, so Inspector Bonilla and his nineteen colleagues plunged on unguided into black arcades of horror that none of them had ever trod before.

The region now entered by the police was one of traditionally evil repute, substantially unknown and untraversed by white men. There were legends of a hidden lake unglimpsed by mortal sight, in which dwelt a huge, formless white polypus thing with luminous eyes; and squatters whispered that bat-winged devils flew up out of caverns in inner earth to worship it at midnight. They said it had been there before d'Iberville, before La Salle, before the Indians, and before even the wholesome beasts and birds of the woods. It was nightmare itself, and to see it was to die. But it made men dream, and so they knew enough to keep away. The present voodoo orgy was, indeed, on the merest fringe of this abhorred area, but that location was bad enough; hence perhaps the very place of the worship had terrified the squatters more than the shocking sounds and incidents.

Only poetry or madness could do justice to the noises heard by Bonilla's men as they ploughed on through the black morass toward the red glare and muffled tom-toms. There are vocal qualities peculiar to men, and vocal qualities peculiar to beasts; and it is terrible to hear the one when the source should yield the other. Animal fury and orgiastic license here whipped themselves to demoniac heights by howls and squawking ecstasies that tore and reverberated through those knighted woods like pestilential tempests from the gulfs of hell. Now and then the less organized ululation would cease, and from what seemed a well-drilled chorus of hoarse voices would rise in sing-song chant that hideous phrase or ritual:

"Ph'nglui mglw'nafh Cthulhu R'lyeh wgah'nagl fhtagn."

Then the men, having reached a spot where the trees were thinner, came suddenly in sight of the spectacle itself. Four of them reeled, one fainted, and two were shaken into a frantic cry which the mad cacophony of the orgy fortunately deadened. Bonilla dashed swamp water on the face of the fainting man, and all stood trembling and nearly hypnotized with horror.

In a natural glade of the swamp stood a grassy island of perhaps an acre's extent, clear of trees and tolerably dry. On this now leaped and twisted a more indescribable horde of human abnormality than any but a Sime or an Angarola could paint. Void of clothing, this hybrid spawn were braying, bellowing, and writhing about a monstrous ring-shaped bonfire; in the center of which, revealed by occasional rifts in the curtain of flame, stood a great granite monolith some eight feet in height; on top of which, incongruous in its diminutiveness, rested the noxious carven statuette.

From a wide circle of ten scaffolds set up at regular intervals with the flame-girt monolith as a center hung, head downward, the oddly marred bodies of the helpless squatters who had disappeared. It was inside this circle that the ring of worshippers jumped and roared, the general direction of the mass motion being from left to right in endless Bacchanal between the ring of bodies and the ring of fire.

It may have been only imagination and it may have been only echoes which induced one of the men, an excitable Spaniard, to fancy he heard antiphonal responses to the ritual from some far and unillumined spot deeper within the wood of ancient legendry and horror. This man, Joseph D. Galvez, I later met and questioned; and he proved distractingly imaginative. He indeed went so far as to hint of the faint beating of great wings, and of a glimpse of shining eyes and a mountainous white bulk beyond the remotest trees but I suppose he had been hearing too much native superstition.

Actually, the horrified pause of the men was of comparatively brief duration. Duty came first; and although there must have been nearly a hundred mongrel celebrants in the throng, the police relied on their firearms and plunged determinedly into the nauseous rout. For five minutes the resultant din and chaos were beyond description. Wild blows were struck, shots were fired, and escapes were made; but in the end Bonilla was able to count some forty-seven sullen prisoners, whom he forced to dress in haste and fall into line between two rows of policemen. Five of the worshippers lay dead, and two severely wounded ones were carried away on improvised stretchers by their fellow-prisoners. The image on the monolith, of course, was carefully removed and carried back by Bonilla."

Mike pulled his backpack from behind the log and plopped it between his legs. His showmanship was as boundless as it was creative. He dove his hand into the backpack and rummaged around for something foreign to the group of friends. His hand navigated with blind ignorance for a few moments, only to come to a complete stop. Mike smirked and slowly pulled his hand out of the backpack. He pulled out an object from the backpack that wasn't readily identifiable to the group.

"See… that monolith, was actually obtained by my Uncle," he said while presenting a doodad to the group.

"Holy shit!", Kevin said abrasively.

Mike passed the monolith around to his friends with an uneasy curiosity. He wasn't sure if they thought it to be real or not. Did this add legitimacy to his tale or detract from it? Time would soon tell. Each member of the group fondled the item. Matt gauged the weight and noted the seemingly authentic nature of the prop. Kevin scrutinized the marking and was taken aback by the realness. Deidra held it for a second only to quickly pass it over to Jon. Jon inspected the angles and quickly passed it back to Mike Allen.

Mike continued, "Examined at headquarters after a trip of intense strain and weariness, the prisoners all proved to be men of a very low, mixed-blooded, and mentally aberrant type. Most were seamen, and a sprinkling of mulattoes, largely West Indians or Brava Portuguese from the Cape Verde Islands, gave a coloring of voodooism to the heterogeneous cult. But before many questions were asked, it became manifest that something far deeper and older than unholy fetishism was involved. Degraded and ignorant as they were, the creatures held with surprising consistency to the central idea of their loathsome faith.

They worshipped, so they said, the *Great Old Ones* who lived ages before there were any men, and who came to the young world out of the sky. Those *Old Ones* were gone now, inside the earth and under the sea; but their dead bodies had told their secrets in dreams to the first men, who formed a cult which had never died. This was that cult, and the prisoners said it had always existed and always would exist, hidden in distant wastes and dark places all over the world until the time when the great priest Cthulhu, from his dark house in the mighty city of R'lyeh under the waters, should rise and bring the earth again beneath his sway. Some day he would call, when the stars were ready, and the secret cult would always be waiting to liberate him.

Meanwhile no more must be told. There was a secret which even torture could not extract. Mankind was not absolutely alone among the conscious things of earth, for shapes came out of the dark to visit the faithful few. But these were not the *Great Old Ones*. No man had ever seen the *Old Ones*. The carven idol was great Cthulhu, but none might say whether or not the others were precisely like him. No one could read the old writing now, but things were told by word of mouth. The chanted ritual was not the secret - that was never spoken aloud, only whispered. The chant meant only this:

"In his house at R'lyeh dead Cthulhu waits dreaming."

"What happened to the prisoners?", Jon asked eagerly.

"What happened?", Mike asked while searching for some additional Smore stuff. Matt quickly picked up on the cue and tossed him some chocolate.

While piecing together his next Smore Mike said, "Only two of the prisoners were found sane enough to be hanged, and the rest were committed to various institutions. All denied a part in the ritual murders, and averred that the killing had been done by Black Winged Ones which had come to them from their immemorial meeting-place in the haunted wood. But of those mysterious allies no coherent account could ever be gained. What the police did extract, came mainly from the immensely aged mestizo named Castro, who claimed to have sailed to strange ports and talked with undying leaders of the cult in the mountains of China."

"Black Winged Ones? That's supposed to scare us? What bats? That's the best you can do? Who believes something like that?", Kevin asked in rapid succession.

"What a bunch of morons," Matt added.

Mike raised his eyebrows as his Smore spontaneously set ablaze. He was unphased by the ignition of his delightful treat. His friends found his normal outgoing personality swapped for an uncharacterizable lugubrious disposition.

"Old Castro, see Old Castro remembered bits of hideous legend that paled the speculations of philosophers and made man and the world seem recent and transient indeed. There had been axons when other *things* ruled on the earth, and *they* had had great cities. Remains of *them*, he said the deathless Chinamen had told him, were still be found as Cyclopean stones on islands in the Pacific. They all died vast epochs of time before men came, but there were arts which could revive Them when the stars had come round again to the right positions in the cycle of eternity. They had, indeed, come themselves from the stars, and brought their images with them.

These *Great Old Ones*, Castro continued, were not composed altogether of flesh and blood. They had shape - for did not this star-fashioned image prove it? - but that shape was not made of matter. When the stars were right, they could plunge from world to world through the sky; but when the stars were wrong, They could not live. But although They no longer lived, They would never really die. They all lay in stone houses in their great city of R'lyeh, preserved by the spells of mighty Cthulhu for a glorious resurrection when the stars and the earth might once more be ready for them. But at that time some force from outside must serve to liberate their bodies. The spells that preserved them intact likewise prevented them from making an initial move, and they could only lie awake in the dark and think whilst uncounted millions of years rolled by. They knew all that was occurring in the universe, for their mode of speech was transmitted thought. Even now they talked in their tombs. When, after infinities of chaos, the first men came, the *Great Old Ones* spoke to the sensitive among them by molding their dreams; for only thus could their language reach the fleshly minds of mammals.

Then, whispered Castro, those first men formed the cult around tall idols which the *Great Ones* shewed them; idols brought in dim eras from dark stars. That cult would never die till the stars came right again, and the secret priests would take great Cthulhu from his tomb to revive his subjects and resume his rule of earth. The time would be easy to know, for then mankind would have become as the *Great Old Ones*; free and wild and beyond good and evil, with laws and morals thrown aside and all men shouting and killing and reveling in joy. Then the liberated *Old Ones* would teach them new ways to shout and kill and revel and enjoy themselves, and all the earth would flame with a holocaust of ecstasy and freedom. Meanwhile the cult, by appropriate rites, must keep alive the memory of those ancient ways and shadow forth the prophecy of their return."

The wind barreled down on the campfire, hurling the flames in dramatic fashion, like the splashes of a baby's bath water during a temper tantrum. Mike took a comb out of his pocket and slicked back his jet-black wavy hair. Deidra's ballcap blew clean off of her head. Kevin, Matt and Jon burst out into spontaneous laughter. Mike looked up at the clouds and sighed.

"What's with the weather?", Matt asked.

"One minute, I'm freezing my balls off, and the next it's as humid as a sauna," Kevin said.

"Yeah… it's unusually warm for this time of year…", Jon noted.

A storm was brewing off the coast of the beach, but the weather forecast showed nothing but clear skies for the evening. The clouds moved as fast and as furious as an out-of-control 1969 Dodge Charger. There was a pale blueish hue to the skyline as the clock approached closer and closer to midnight. Deidra grabbed a blanket from her backpack and swung it over her head.

"Drinks?", Jon asked.

Without compunction the group said in unison, "Drinks!"

Jon pushed up his glasses and searched around for the ice-chest. The ice-chest was bright red, and constructed of heavily insulated plastic. Under the natural lighting of the sky, the container was a hazy purple. Jon grabbed the ice-chest and slid it front of his feet. He propped open the ice-chest to find a full cadre of off-label beer. Jon plucked various beers out of the ice-chest and tossed them around like a waitress flinging cigarette carton's at the Playboy Lounge.

Mike cracked open a beer and continued his story, "In the elder time chosen men had talked with the entombed *Old Ones* in dreams, but then something happened. The great stone city R'lyeh, with its monoliths and sepulchers, had sunk beneath the waves; and the deep waters, full of the one primal mystery through which not even thought can pass, had cut off the spectral intercourse. But memory never died, and the high-priests said that the city would rise again *when the stars were right*. Then came out of the earth the black spirits of earth, moldy and shadowy, and full of dim rumors picked up in caverns beneath forgotten sea-bottoms. But of them old Castro dared not speak much. He cut himself off hurriedly, and no amount of persuasion or subtlety could elicit more in this direction. The size of the *Old Ones*, too, he curiously declined to mention. Of the cult, he said that he thought the center lay amid the pathless desert of Arabia, where Ire, the City of Pillars, dreams hidden and untouched. It was not allied to the European witch-cult, and was virtually unknown beyond its members. No book had ever really hinted of it, though the deathless Chinamen said that there were double meanings in the Necronomicon of the mad Arab Abdul Alhazred which the initiated might read as they chose, especially the much-discussed couplet:

That is not dead which can eternally lie, And with strange axons even death may die."

"Even *death* may die…", Mike said while taking a moment to chug his beer.

The rest of the group hoisted up their beers and said, "Even death may die!"

Mike slammed down his beer can and said, "Bonilla, deeply impressed and not a little bewildered, had inquired in vain concerning the historic affiliations of the cult. Castro, apparently, had told the truth when he said that it was wholly secret. The authorities at Tulane University could shed no light upon either cult or image, and now the detective had come to the highest authorities in the country and met with no more than the Greenland tale of Professor Webb.

The feverish interest aroused at the meeting by Bonilla's tale, corroborated as it was by the statuette, is echoed in the subsequent correspondence of those who attended; although scant mention occurs in the formal publications of the society. Caution is the first care of those accustomed to face occasional charlatanry and imposture. Bonilla for some time lent the image to Professor Webb, but at the latter's death it was returned to him and remains in his possession, where I viewed it not long ago. It is truly a terrible thing, and unmistakably akin to the dream-sculpture of young Wilcox.

That my uncle was excited by the tale of the sculptor I did not wonder, for what thoughts must arise upon hearing, after a knowledge of what Bonilla had learned of the cult, of a sensitive young man who had dreamed not only the figure and exact hieroglyphics of the swamp-found image and the Greenland devil tablet, but had come in his dreams upon at least three of the precise words of the formula uttered alike by Esquimaux diabolists and mongrel Louisianans? Professor Hodges's instant start on an investigation of the utmost thoroughness was eminently natural; though privately I suspected young Wilcox of having heard of the cult in some indirect way, and of having invented a series of dreams to heighten and continue the mystery at my uncle's expense. The dream-narratives and cuttings collected by the professor were, of course, strong corroboration; but the rationalism of my mind and the extravagance of the whole subject led me to adopt what I thought the most sensible conclusions. So, after thoroughly studying the manuscript again and correlating the philosophical and anthropological notes with the cult narrative of Bonilla, I made a trip to Providence to see the sculptor and give him the rebuke I thought proper for so boldly imposing upon a learned and aged man.

Wilcox still lived alone in the Fleur-de-Lys Building in Thomas Street, a hideous Victorian imitation of seventeenth century Breton Architecture which flaunts its stucco exterior amidst the lovely colonial houses on the ancient hill, and under the very shadow of the finest Georgian steeple in America, I found him at work in his rooms, and at once conceded from the specimens scattered about that his genius is indeed profound and authentic. He will, I believe, sometime be heard from as one of the great decadents; for he has crystallized in clay and will one day mirror in marble those nightmares and phantasies which Arthur Machen evokes in prose, and Clark Ashton Smith makes visible in verse and in painting.

Dark, frail, and somewhat unkempt in aspect, he turned languidly at my knock and asked me my business without rising. Then I told him who I was, he displayed some interest; for my uncle had excited his curiosity in probing his strange dreams, yet had never explained the reason for the study. I did not enlarge his knowledge in this regard, but sought with some subtlety to draw him out. In a short time I became convinced of his absolute sincerity, for he spoke of the dreams in a manner none could mistake. They and their subconscious residuum had influenced his art profoundly, and he shewed me a morbid statue whose contours almost made me shake with the potency of its black suggestion. He could not recall having seen the original of this thing except in his own dream bas-relief, but the outlines had formed themselves insensibly under his hands. It was, no doubt, the giant shape he had raved of in delirium. That he really knew nothing of the hidden cult, save from what my uncle's relentless catechism had let fall, he soon made clear; and again I strove to think of some way in which he could possibly have received the weird impressions.

He talked of his dreams in a strangely poetic fashion; making me see with terrible vividness the damp Cyclopean city of slimy green stone - whose geometry, he oddly said, was all wrong – and hear with frightened expectancy the ceaseless, half-mental calling from underground:

"Cthulhu fhtagn", "Cthulhu fhtagn."

These words had formed part of that dread ritual which told of dead Cthulhu's dream-vigil in his stone vault at R'lyeh, and I felt deeply moved despite my rational beliefs. Wilcox, I was sure, had heard of the cult in some casual way, and had soon forgotten it amidst the mass of his equally weird reading and imagining. Later, by virtue of its sheer impressiveness, it had found subconscious expression in dreams, in the bas-relief, and in the terrible statue I now beheld; so that his imposture upon my uncle had been a very innocent one. The youth was of a type, at once slightly affected and slightly ill-mannered, which I could never like, but I was willing enough now to admit both his genius and his honesty. I took leave of him amicably, and wish him all the success his talent promises.

The matter of the cult still remained to fascinate me, and at times I had visions of personal fame from researches into its origin and connexons. I visited New Orleans, talked with Bonilla and others of that old-time raiding-party, saw the frightful image, and even questioned such of the mongrel prisoners as still survived. Old Castro, unfortunately, had been dead for some years. What I now heard so graphically at first-hand, though it was really no more than a detailed confirmation of what my uncle had written, excited me afresh; for I felt sure that I was on the track of a very real, very secret, and very ancient religion whose discovery would make me an anthropologist of note. My attitude was still one of absolute materialism, as I wish it still were, and I discounted with almost inexplicable perversity the coincidence of the dream notes and odd cuttings collected by Professor Hodges.

One thing I began to suspect, and which I now fear I know, is that my uncle's death was far from natural. He fell on a narrow hill street leading up from an ancient waterfront swarming with foreign mongrels, after a careless push from a sailor. I did not forget the mixed blood and marine pursuits of the cult-members in Louisiana, and would not be surprised to learn of secret methods and rites and beliefs. Bonilla and his men, it is true, have been let alone; but in Norway a certain seaman who saw things is dead. Might not the deeper inquiries of my uncle after encountering the sculptor's data have come to sinister ears?. I think Professor Hodges died because he knew too much, or because he was likely to learn too much. Whether I shall go as he did remains to be seen, for I have learned much now…"

The salty sea water splashed sludge onto the shore with a calamitous frequency. Each wave plastered the shoreline of the *Mohegan Bluffs*, like the thunderous blows of a heavyweight boxer pounding a side of beef. As Mike turned his head toward the shoreline, his collar dropped down just enough to reveal a tattoo.

"No *way*! When did *Mike Allen* get a tattoo?", Kevin asked to his friend while pointing at his neck.

"What is it?", Matt asked with a curious gaze.

"I *don't* believe it!", Deidra shouted alongside her equally perplexed compatriots.

Mike clandestinely covered up his neck by nonchalantly pulling up his collar. His neck adorned a series of discontinuous jet-black tattoos stemming from his collar bone up to the base of his skull. The group couldn't make heads or tails of the design. Mike wasn't too keen on talking about it, like the stolidness of a *Queen's Guard* standing at attention outside of *Buckingham Palace*.

Mike continued his bantam banter, "If heaven ever wishes to grant me a boon, it will be a total effacing of the results of a mere chance which fixed my eye on a certain stray piece of shelf-paper. It was nothing on which I would naturally have stumbled in the course of my daily round, for it was an old number of an Australian journal, the Sydney Bulletin for April 18, 1925. It had escaped even the cutting bureau which had at the time of its issuance been avidly collecting material for my uncle's research.

I had largely given over my inquiries into what Professor Hodges called the "*Cthulhu Cult*", and was visiting a learned friend in Paterson, New Jersey; the curator of a local museum and a mineralogist of note. Examining one day the reserve specimens roughly set on the storage shelves in a rear room of the museum, my eye was caught by an odd picture in one of the old papers spread beneath the stones. It was the Sydney Bulletin I have mentioned, for my friend had wide affiliations in all conceivable foreign parts; and the picture was a half-tone cut of a hideous stone image almost identical with that which Bonilla had found in the swamp.

Eagerly clearing the sheet of its precious contents, I scanned the item in detail; and was disappointed to find it of only moderate length. What it suggested, however, was of portentous significance to my flagging quest; and I carefully tore it out for immediate action. It read as follows:

MYSTERY DERELICT FOUND AT SEA

Vigilant Arrives With Helpless Armed New Zealand Yacht in Tow. One Survivor and Dead Man Found Aboard. Tale of Desperate Battle and Deaths at Sea. Rescued Seaman Refuses Particulars of Strange Experience. Odd Idol Found in His Possession. Inquiry to Follow.

The Morrison Co.'s freighter Vigilant, bound from Valparaiso, arrived this morning at its wharf in Darling Harbor, having in tow the battled and disabled but heavily armed steam yacht Alert of Dunedin, N.Z., which was sighted April 12th in S. Latitude 34°21', W. Longitude 152°17', with one living and one dead man aboard.

The Vigilant left Valparaiso March 25th, and on April 2nd was driven considerably south of her course by exceptionally heavy storms and monster waves. On April 12th the derelict was sighted; and though apparently deserted, was found upon boarding to contain one survivor in a half-delirious condition and one man who had evidently been dead for more than a week. The living man was clutching a horrible stone idol of unknown origin, about foot in height, regarding whose nature authorities at Sydney University, the Royal Society, and the Museum in College Street all profess complete bafflement, and which the survivor says he found in the cabin of the yacht, in a small carved shrine of common pattern.

This man, after recovering his senses, told an exceedingly strange story of piracy and slaughter. He is Gustaf Johansen, a Norwegian of some intelligence, and had been second mate of the two-masted schooner Emma of Auckland, which sailed for Callao February 20th with a complement of eleven men. The Emma, he says, was delayed and thrown widely south of her course by the great storm of March 1st, and on March 22nd, in S. Latitude 49°51' W. Longitude 128°34', encountered the Alert, manned by a queer and evil-looking crew of Kanakas and half-castes. Being ordered peremptorily to turn back, Capt. Collins refused; whereupon the strange crew began to fire savagely and without warning upon the schooner with a peculiarly heavy battery of brass cannon forming part of the yacht's equipment. The Emma 's men shewed fight, says the survivor, and though the schooner began to sink from shots beneath the water-line they managed to heave alongside their enemy and board her, grappling with the savage crew on the yacht's deck, and being forced to kill them all, the number being slightly superior, because of their particularly abhorrent and desperate though rather clumsy mode of fighting.

Three of the Emma's men, including Capt. Collins and First Mate Green, were killed; and the remaining eight under Second Mate Johansen proceeded to navigate the captured yacht, going ahead in their original direction to see if any reason for their ordering back had existed. The next day, it appears, they raised and landed on a small island, although none is known to exist in that part of the ocean; and six of the men somehow died ashore, though Johansen is queerly reticent about this part of his story, and speaks only of their falling into a rock chasm. Later, it seems, he and one companion boarded the yacht and tried to manage her, but were beaten about by the storm of April 2nd, From that time till his rescue on the 12th the man remembers little, and he does not even recall when William Joe Brandon, his companion, died. Brandon's death reveals no apparent cause, and was probably due to excitement or exposure. Cable advices from Dunedin report that the Alert was well known there as an island trader, and bore an evil reputation along the waterfront, It was owned by a curious group of half-castes whose frequent meetings and night trips to the woods attracted no little curiosity; and it had set sail in great haste just after the storm and earth tremors of March 1st. Our Auckland correspondent gives the Emma and her crew an excellent reputation, and Johansen is described as a sober and worthy man. The admiralty will institute an inquiry on the whole matter beginning tomorrow, at which every effort will be made to induce Johansen to speak more freely than he has done hitherto.

This was all, together with the picture of the hellish image; but what a train of ideas it started in my mind! Here were new treasuries of data on the *Cthulhu Cult*, and evidence that it had strange interests at sea as well as on land. What motive prompted the hybrid crew to order back the

Emma as they sailed about with their hideous idol? What was the unknown island on which six of the Emma 's crew had died, and about which the mate Johansen was so secretive? What had the vice-admiralty's investigation brought out, and what was known of the noxious cult in Dunedin? And most marvelous of all, what deep and more than natural linkage of dates was this which gave a malign and now undeniable significance to the various turns of events so carefully noted by my uncle?

March 1st - or February 28th according to the International Date Line - the earthquake and storm had come. From Dunedin the Alert and her noisome crew had darted eagerly forth as if imperiously summoned, and on the other side of the earth poets and artists had begun to dream of a strange, dank Cyclopean city whilst a young sculptor had molded in his sleep the form of the dreaded Cthulhu. March 23rd the crew of the Emma landed on an unknown island and left six men dead; and on that date the dreams of sensitive men assumed a heightened vividness and darkened with dread of a giant monster's malign pursuit, whilst an architect had gone mad and a sculptor had lapsed suddenly into delirium! And what of this storm of April 2nd - the date on which all dreams of the dank city ceased, and Wilcox emerged unharmed from the bondage of strange fever? What of all this - and of those hints of old Castro about the sunken, star-born Old Ones and their coming reign; their faithful cult and their mastery of dreams? Was I tottering on the brink of cosmic horrors beyond man's power to bear? If so, they must be horrors of the mind alone, for in some way the second of April had put a stop to whatever monstrous menace had begun its siege of mankind's soul. That evening, after a day of hurried cabling and arranging, I bade my host adieu and took a train for San Francisco. In less than a month I was in Dunedin; where, however, I found that little was known of the strange cult-members who had lingered in the old sea-taverns. Waterfront scum was far too common for special mention; though there was vague talk about one inland trip these mongrels had made, during which faint drumming and red flame were noted on the distant hills. In Auckland I learned that Johansen had returned with yellow hair turned white after a perfunctory and inconclusive questioning at Sydney, and had thereafter sold his cottage in West Street and sailed with his wife to his old home in Oslo. Of his stirring experience he would tell his friends no more than he had told the admiralty officials, and all they could do was to give me his Oslo address.

After that I went to Sydney and talked profitlessly with seamen and members of the vice-admiralty court. I saw the Alert, now sold and in commercial use, at Circular Quay in Sydney Cove, but gained nothing from its non-committal bulk. The crouching image with its cuttlefish head, dragon body, scaly wings, and hieroglyphed pedestal, was preserved in the Museum at Hyde Park; and I studied it long and well, finding it a thing of balefully exquisite workmanship, and with the same utter mystery, terrible antiquity, and unearthly strangeness of material which I had noted in Bonilla's smaller specimen. Geologists, the curator told me, had found it a monstrous puzzle; for they vowed that the world held no rock like it. Then I thought with a shudder of what Old Castro had told Bonilla about the Old Ones; "They had come from the stars, and had brought Their images with Them."

Shaken with such a mental revolution as I had never before known, I now resolved to visit Mate Johansen in Oslo. Sailing for London, I reembarked at once for the Norwegian capital; and one autumn day landed at the trim wharves in the shadow of the Egeberg. Johansen's address, I discovered, lay in the Old Town of King Harold Haardrada, which kept alive the name of Oslo during all the centuries that the greater city masqueraded as "Christiana." I made the brief trip by taxicab, and knocked with palpitant heart at the door of a neat and ancient building with plastered front. A sad-faced woman in black answered my summons, and I was stung with disappointment when she told me in halting English that Gustaf Johansen was no more.

He had not long survived his return, said his wife, for the doings sea in 1925 had broken him. He had told her no more than he told the public, but had left a long manuscript - of "technical matters" as he said - written in English, evidently in order to guard her from the peril of casual perusal. During a walk through a narrow lane near the Gothenburg dock, a bundle of papers falling from an attic window had knocked him down. Two Lascar sailors at once helped him to his feet, but before the ambulance could reach him he was dead. Physicians found no adequate cause the end, and laid it to heart trouble and a weakened constitution. I now felt gnawing at my vitals that dark terror which will never leave me till I, too, am at rest; "accidentally" or otherwise. Persuading the widow that my connexon with her husband's "technical matters" was sufficient to entitle me to his manuscript, I bore the document away and began to read it on the London boat.

It was a simple, rambling thing - a naive sailor's effort at a post-facto diary - and strove to recall day by day that last awful voyage. I cannot attempt to transcribe it verbatim in all its cloudiness and redundance, but I will tell its gist enough to shew why the sound the water against the vessel's sides became so unendurable to me that I stopped my ears with cotton.

Johansen, thank God, did not know quite all, even though he saw the city and the Thing, but I shall never sleep calmly again when I think of the horrors that lurk ceaselessly behind life in time and in space, and of those unhallowed blasphemies from elder stars which dream beneath the sea, known and favored by a nightmare cult ready and eager to lose them upon the world whenever another earthquake shall heave their monstrous stone city again to the sun and air.

Johansen's voyage had begun just as he told it to the vice-admiralty. The Emma, in ballast, had cleared Auckland on February 20th, and had felt the full force of that earthquake-born tempest which must have heaved up from the sea-bottom the horrors that filled men's dreams. Once more under control, the ship was making good progress when held up by the Alert on March 22nd, and I could feel the mate's regret as he wrote of her bombardment and sinking. Of the swarthy cult-fiends on the Alert he speaks with significant horror. There was some peculiarly abominable quality about them which made their destruction seem almost a duty, and Johansen shews ingenuous wonder at the charge of ruthlessness brought against his party during the proceedings of the court of inquiry. Then, driven ahead by curiosity in their captured yacht under Johansen's command, the men sight a great stone pillar sticking out of the sea, and in S. Latitude 47°9', W. Longitude 123°43', come upon a coastline of mingled mud, ooze, and weedy Cyclopean masonry which can be nothing less than the tangible substance of earth's supreme terror - the nightmare corpse-city of R'lyeh, that was built in measureless axons behind history by the vast, loathsome shapes that seeped down from the dark stars. There lay great Cthulhu and his hordes, hidden in green slimy vaults and sending out at last, after cycles incalculable, the thoughts that spread fear to the dreams of the sensitive and called imperiously to the faithful to come on a pilgrimage of liberation and restoration. All this Johansen did not suspect, but God knows he soon saw enough!

I suppose that only a single mountain-top, the hideous monolith-crowned citadel whereon great Cthulhu was buried, actually emerged from the waters. When I think of the extent of all that may be brooding down there I almost wish to kill myself forthwith. Johansen and his men were awed by the cosmic majesty of this dripping Babylon of elder daemons, and must have guessed without guidance that it was nothing of this or of any sane planet. Awe at the unbelievable size of the greenish stone blocks, at the dizzying height of the great carven monolith, and at the stupefying identity of the colossal statues and bas-reliefs with the queer image found in the shrine on the Alert, is poignantly visible in every line of the mates frightened description.

Without knowing what futurism is like, Johansen achieved something very close to it when he spoke of the city; for instead of describing any definite structure or building, he dwells only on broad impressions of vast angles and stone surfaces - surfaces too great to belong to anything right or proper for this earth, and impious with horrible images and hieroglyphs. I mention his talk about angles because it suggests something Wilcox had told me of his awful dreams. He said that the geometry of the dream-place he saw was abnormal, non-Euclidean, and loathsomely redolent of spheres and dimensions apart from ours. Now an unlettered seaman felt the same thing whilst gazing at the terrible reality.

Johansen and his men landed at a sloping mud-bank on this monstrous Acropolis, and clambered slippery up over titan oozy blocks which could have been no mortal staircase. The very sun of heaven seemed distorted when viewed through the polarizing miasma welling out from this sea-soaked perversion, and twisted menace and suspense lurked leeringly in those crazily elusive angles of carven rock where a second glance shewed concavity after the first shewed convexity.

Something very like fright had come over all the explorers before anything more definite than rock and ooze and weed was seen. Each would have fled had he not feared the scorn of the others, and it was only half-heartedly that they searched - vainly, as it proved - for some portable souvenir to bear away.

It was Rodriguez the Portuguese who climbed up the foot of the monolith and shouted of what he had found. The rest followed him, and looked curiously at the immense carved door with the now familiar squid-dragon bas-relief. It was, Johansen said, like a great barn-door; and they all felt that it was a door because of the ornate lintel, threshold, and jambs around it, though they could not decide whether it lay flat like a trap-door or slantwise like an outside cellar-door. As Wilcox would have said, the geometry of the place was all wrong. One could not be sure that the sea and the ground were horizontal, hence the relative position of everything else seemed phantasmal in nature.

Brandon pushed at the stone in several places without result. Then Donovan felt over it delicately around the edge, pressing each point separately as he went. He climbed interminably along the grotesque stone molding - that is, one would call it climbing if the thing was not after all horizontal - and the men wondered how any door in the universe could be so vast. Then, very softly and slowly, the acre-great lintel began to give inward at the top; and they saw that it was balanced.

Donovan slid or somehow propelled himself down or along the jamb and rejoined his fellows, and everyone watched the queer recession of the monstrously carven portal. In this phantasy of prismatic distortion it moved anomalously in a diagonal way, so that all the rules of matter and perspective seemed upset.

The aperture was black with a darkness almost material. That tenebrousness was indeed a positive quality; for it obscured such parts of the inner walls as ought to have been revealed, and actually burst forth like smoke from its Aeon-long imprisonment, visibly darkening the sun as it slunk away into the shrunken and gibbous sky on flapping membranous wings. The odor rising from the newly opened depths was intolerable, and at length the quick-eared Hawkins thought he heard a nasty, slopping sound down there. Everyone listened, and everyone was listening still when It lumbered slobbering into sight and gropingly squeezed Its gelatinous green immensity through the black doorway into the tainted outside air of that poison city of madness.

Poor Johansen's handwriting almost gave out when he wrote of this. Of the six men who never reached the ship, he thinks two perished of pure fright in that accursed instant. The Thing cannot be described - there is no language for such abysms of shrieking and immemorial lunacy, such eldritch contradictions of all matter, force, and cosmic order. A mountain walked or stumbled. God! What wonder that across the earth a great architect went mad, and poor Wilcox raved with fever in that telepathic instant? The Thing of the idols, the green, sticky spawn of the stars, had awaked to claim his own. The stars were right again, and what an age-old cult had failed to do by design, a band of innocent sailors had done by accident. After vigintillions of years great Cthulhu was loose again, and ravening for delight.

Three men were swept up by the flabby claws before anybody turned. God rest them, if there be any rest in the universe. They were Donovan, Guerrera, and Angstrom. Parker slipped as the other three were plunging frenziedly over endless vistas of green-crusted rock to the boat, and Johansen swears he was swallowed up by an angle of masonry which shouldn't have been there; an angle which was acute, but behaved as if it were obtuse. So only Brandon and Johansen reached the boat, and pulled desperately for the Alert as the mountainous monstrosity flopped down the slimy stones and hesitated, floundering at the edge of the water.

Steam had not been suffered to go down entirely, despite the departure of all hands for the shore; and it was the work of only a few moments of feverish rushing up and down between wheel and engines to get the Alert under way. Slowly, amidst the distorted horrors of that indescribable scene, she began to churn the lethal waters; whilst on the masonry of that charnel shore that was not of earth the titan Thing from the stars slavered and gibbered like Polypheme cursing the fleeing ship of Odysseus. Then, bolder than the storied Cyclops, great Cthulhu slid greasily into the water and began to pursue with vast wave-raising strokes of cosmic potency. Brandon looked back and went mad, laughing shrilly as he kept on laughing at intervals till death found him one night in the cabin whilst Johansen was wandering deliriously.

But Johansen had not given out yet. Knowing that the Thing could surely overtake the Alert until steam was fully up, he resolved on a desperate chance; and, setting the engine for full speed, ran lightning-like on deck and reversed the wheel. There was a mighty eddying and foaming in the noisome brine, and as the steam mounted higher and higher the brave Norwegian drove his vessel head on against the pursuing jelly which rose above the unclean froth like the stern of a daemon galleon. The awful squid-head with writhing feelers came nearly up to the bowsprit of the sturdy yacht, but Johansen drove on relentlessly. There was a bursting as of an exploding bladder, a slushy nastiness as of a cloven sunfish, a stench as of a thousand opened graves, and a sound that the chronicler could not put on paper. For an instant the ship was befouled by an acrid and blinding green cloud, and then there was only a venomous seething astern; where - God in heaven! - the scattered plasticity of that nameless sky-spawn was nebulously recombining in its hateful original form, whilst its distance widened every second as the Alert gained impetus from its mounting steam.

That was all. After that Johansen only brooded over the idol in the cabin and attended to a few matters of food for himself and the laughing maniac by his side. He did not try to navigate after the first bold flight, for the reaction had taken something out of his soul.

Then came the storm of April 2nd, and a gathering of the clouds about his consciousness. There is a sense of spectral whirling through liquid gulfs of infinity, of dizzying rides through reeling universes on a comets tail, and of hysterical plunges from the pit to the moon and from the moon back again to the pit, all livened by a cachinnating chorus of the distorted, hilarious elder gods and the green, bat-winged mocking imps of Tartarus.

Out of that dream came rescue-the Vigilant, the vice-admiralty court, the streets of Dunedin, and the long voyage back home to the old house by the Egeberg. He could not tell - they would think him mad. He would write of what he knew before death came, but his wife must not guess. Death would be a boon if only it could blot out the memories.

That was the document I read, and now I have placed it in the tin box beside the bas-relief and the papers of Professor Hodges. With it shall go this record of mine - this test of my own sanity, wherein is pieced together that which I hope may never be pieced together again. I have looked upon all that the universe has to hold of horror, and even the skies of spring and the flowers of summer must ever afterward be poison to me. But I do not think my life will be long. As my uncle went, as poor Johansen went, so I shall go. I know too much, and the cult still lives.

Cthulhu still lives, too, I suppose, again in that chasm of stone which has shielded him since the sun was young. His accursed city is sunken once more, for the Vigilant sailed over the spot after the April storm; but his ministers on earth still bellow and prance and slay around idol-capped monoliths in lonely places. He must have been trapped by the sinking whilst within his black abyss, or else the world would by now be screaming with fright and frenzy. Who knows the end? What has risen may sink, and what has sunk may rise. Loathsomeness waits and dreams in the deep, and decay spreads over the tottering cities of men. A time will come - but I must not and cannot think! Let me pray that, if I do not survive this manuscript, my executors may put caution before audacity and see that it meets no other eye.

"The end…"

Clap. Clap. Clap. Clap.

"Hell of a story, buddy," Kevin said while continuing his slow clap.

"Not bad, my guy," Matt said while crushing his beer can between his hands.

"I've been looking for the right time to tell that one… The moon had to be *just* right…", Mike said while staring up at the sky with a melancholic magnetism.

Clouds began to roll in over the shoreline from the outer banks, like plumes from fog machines canvasing a concert stage. A flock of seagulls began to squawk uncontrollably, like a bunch of car alarms randomly going off in a parking lot. Suddenly, the rambunctious seagulls silently scattered in to every direction.

"What's so special about tonight?", Deidra asked.

Mike reached down and plunged his hand into the chunky sand. He pulled away his sandy hand and said, "See… tonight's full moon isn't like an ordinary full moon. Tonight, Mercury is in retrograde…"

A deafening series of tectonic thuds reverberated the ground, like the lumbering feint tremble after a *Rocket Launch* at *Cape Canaveral*. The logs began to sway back and forth, like the hypnotic dance of a *Houla-Girl* flaunting her rotund hips at a *Luau*. Kevin attempted to jolt up from his seat, but was met with a relentless quake. After a few failed attempts, he was able to get to his feet.

"Earthquake!?!?", Jon shouted.

The trees violently shook, like a Whacky-arm-flailing-inflatable-tube-man gyrating in a wind tunnel. Mike rose from his seat completely unmolested by the shaking. He pulled out a jagged knife from his waist. He effortlessly slid the knife across the palm of his hand, like the smooth motion of buttering a warm roll. Blood oozed over the monolith, like caramel hot fudge smothering an ice cream sundae. Mike tossed the knife into the sand and lathered the monolith with both hands. He held the blood laden monolith up to the sky and shouted:

"Ph'nglui mglw'nafh Cthulhu R'lyeh wgah'nagl fhtagn."

The water began to secede from the beachfront back into the ocean, like the preceding drainage only accompanied by an oncoming Tsunami. Fish flopped about on the newly exposed shoreline. The winds ungulated with a furious hollow. The Earth around the campfire shook harder than a crack addict spasming in withdrawal. The ensemble looked over to Mike with terror as he shouted, and shouted again, *"Ph'nglui mglw'nafh Cthulhu R'lyeh wgah'nagl fhtagn!"*

The End

This novel is the fourth installation by Lorenzo di Toni, in the "*The 12 Labours of Mike Allen*", which can all be found on Amazon or Audible. The series was developed out of 12 life lessons that I learned the hard way. Ultimately, when I started writing Flushy back in 2017, it was no more than an outlet for destressing. Over time, it became a labor of love for me. Flushy re-ignited my passion for writing and telling stories. Sharing stories is a tradition handed down by every culture going back throughout human history. If you're interested in supporting my work, please check out some of the other books in my series.

1. **Flushy: A Tale of Corporate Satire in the Insurance Industry**: The Insure-tech industry has become an overnight sensation and darling of Wall Street. In the span of a decade the Insure-tech industry has become a Ten Billion Dollar behemoth. Leading the way is a fast up-start Insure-tech plainly named Flushy. In the blink of an eye, Flushy has become the most powerful Insure-Tech of them all. Flushy set out to up-end the entire insurance industry and become the world's first insurance carrier to be valued at One Trillion dollars. "Flushy: A Tale of Corporate Satire in the Insurance Industry" follows our main character Mike Allen through the ups and downs of his insurance career. Mike Allen gets easily wrapped up in the glitz and glamor of this niche, but booming industry. At Flushy, some people float to the top, some sink to the bottom, but in the end they all get flushed. Mike Allen tests that very proposition as a

young money-hungry insurance executive thrust into a prominent role in the corporate toilet bowl.

2. **Escape from Plum Island**: In the world of Special Operations Warfare there is no margin for error. That is a lesson that is all too familiar for the Marine Recon regiment stationed at Fort Lejeune. Escape from Plum Island follows First Sergeant Mike Allen, a former insurance guru turned Special Operator, as he is plunged head first into the vanguard of Spec Ops. Sergeant Allen is tasked with leading a Special Reconnaissance mission into one of the deadliest battle grounds known to man.

3. **Murder on the Mary:** The Queen Mary was launched in 1934 and served as a transatlantic liner, troop transport, and cruise ship until it was mysteriously moored in 1967 at the port of Long Beach, California. On October 31st 1967 the Queen Mary unknowingly sailed its final and deadly voyage from London to Long Beach. The Queen embarked on its 1000th voyage across the Atlantic Ocean. Unexpectedly, more than 12 passengers paid an unexpected toll, a deadly toll. In this Historical Fiction, we follow our main character Mike Allen throughout his journey of modern exploration on the Queen Mary. Mike quickly makes the company of a young concierge named Katharina, who he avails on his journey. The two are deadest for a flash in the pan romp on the Queen Mary, but soon find out that they both might have gotten more than they bargained for.

4. **The Tale of Cthulhu:** On nights when the moon is full, a small group of high-school friends gather around a campfire near the *Mohegan Bluffs*. On nights when the moon is full, they unleash

ancient terrors. On nights when the moon is full, they share the sacred art of storytelling. On this night, the moon is as full as the stories are terrifying. For on this harrowing night in *New England*, Mike Allen will tell a story as old as mankind itself. This particular story has been passed down from generation to generation, with caution interwoven into every spoken word. On this night, they make a call to the old gods. On this night, they make a call to the cult that never died. On this night, they make a call to… *Cthulhu.*